Jim Henson presents

The Tale of the Bunny Picnic

By Louise Gikow Illustrated by Diane Dawson Hearn

Based on the television show by Jocelyn Stevenson

ISBN 0-590-40837-2

12 11 10 9 8 7 6 5 4 3 2

7 8 9/8 0 1 2/9

Printed in the U.S.A.
First Scholastic printing, March 1987

23

SCHOLASTIC INC.

New York   Toronto   London   Auckland   Sydney

As Any Bunny can tell you, the most wonderful thing about being a bunny is the Bunny Picnic.

The Bunny Picnic happens once a year, just as spring begins to cover the fields and meadows with daisies, primroses, and fresh green grass. It's the time when bunnies hop out of their burrows to celebrate the end of the long, cold winter.

This year was no different. Bunnies scampered about, putting up decorations, baking yummy bunny treats, and watching for the arrival of the storyteller bunny. Without the storyteller, the Bunny Picnic simply wouldn't be the Bunny Picnic.

Bean Bunny stood for a moment, sniffing the sweet spring breezes and watching with admiration as his big sister Twitch and his even bigger brother Lugsy finished weaving a flower garland of bluebells and dandelions. Then he hurried over to help.

"Hey, wait for me!" Bean shouted and waved as Lugsy started to hang the garland on the oak tree that stood by the entrance to the burrow.

Bean hopped toward his brother. On the way, he tripped over a root in the ground. The next thing he knew, he had rolled right into Lugsy — knocking both him and the garland down. The garland settled neatly on Lugsy's head.

"I'm sorry, Lugsy," Bean panted. "I was trying to hurry."

"Well, hurry somewhere else," Lugsy said, shaking the garland off his head.

Bean's ears slowly drooped. "Please, Lugsy," he begged. "I want to help you. Isn't there anything I can do?"

"Yes," Lugsy replied. "You can LEAVE!"

Bean Bunny's ears drooped even more. Slowly, he hopped away, a small tear trickling down his nose. *Lugsy*

thinks I can't do anything, he thought, squeezing through the hedge and into the lettuce patch. *But I can! I'm not a little bunny at all. I'm really a giant...a giant eagle! I can pick up that garland in my giant claws and hang it on the tree just like that!*

Or if anything horrible, awful, and terrible happened to Lugsy, I could rescue him! And then he'd see....

Bean stopped short. He gasped, and his eyes opened wide in fear. There, not ten feet away, was something more horrible, awful, and terrible than he ever could have imagined.

It was a Dog.

"Hellllllp!"

Bean Bunny bolted through the hedge and ran past Lugsy and Twitch and straight for home.

"What is the matter with that batty little bunny?" Lugsy asked Twitch.

"I don't know," Twitch replied. "But we'd better go and find out."

Lugsy and Twitch found Bean hiding under his bed.

"Bean? Is that you?" Lugsy asked, picking up the corner of Bean's bedspread.

"No," came a deep voice. "It's a giant fire-breathing dragon!"

"What?"

"I'm a fire-breathing dragon. No Dog's gonna get me now!"

"What are you talking about, Bean?" Twitch asked, poking her nose under the bed.

"A Dog." Bean shuddered. "In the lettuce patch! It was the most horrible, awful, terrible thing I've ever seen!"

"Come on, Bean," Lugsy said impatiently. "Every bunny knows that the Farmer hates Dogs. The last time any bunny saw a Dog around here was way before we were born!"

"Well, I saw one just now," insisted Bean.

"Yeah," Lugsy said, shaking his head. "Just like you're a fire-breathing dragon."

"Twitch! Lugsy! Bean!" Mother's voice floated into the room. "Could you come here a minute, please?"

"Coming!" Lugsy called back.

"Not me." Bean shook his head. "I'm not leaving this room!"

"Oh, yes you are." Lugsy grabbed Bean by the paw. "Mother called all of us. Besides, a fire-breathing dragon like you might come in real handy!"

"Pickled parsnips," Mother was saying. "We've looked everywhere, and there's none to be found. And you know we can't make our traditional Bunny Picnic pies without pickled parsnips! Will you three hop across the meadow to Great-great-great-great-grandmother's house and borrow some?"

"No problem," answered Lugsy.

"Easy-peasy-one-two-threesy!" added Twitch.

"Never!" declared Bean.

"Why not?" Mother asked.

"There's a Dog out there!" Bean quaked.

"Did you say Dog?" Father asked, starting to tremble. Father had seen a Dog once, many years before, and he had never gotten over it.

"Yes, he did, Father," said Lugsy. "But it's just his imagination...again."

"It is not!" Bean protested, but Lugsy and Twitch were already hurrying him out the door.

"Hello, Great-great-great-great-grandbunnies!"

Great-great-great-great-grandmother stood in the door-way of her house. A delicious scent drifted around her and into the noses of the three bunnies.

"Hello, Great-great-great-great-grandmother," they said.

"That smells wonderful!" Twitch added.

"It's my latest magic potion," Grannie explained. "I'm mixing a hopping potion with a sleeping potion so you can hop out of bed in the morning while you're still in dreamland. But don't get any on your whiskers. I've just finished the sleeping potion. If you tasted just a tiny bit, you'd fall asleep in a minute!

"So, Lugsy," Grannie went on as the bunnies filed into

her burrow. "You've got your ears all in a twist about young Bean here." Grannie always seemed to know what was going on before anyone told her.

"He says he saw a Dog," Lugsy sniffed. "Can you believe it?"

"Well," said Grannie, scratching behind her left ear, "I have ninety-five grandchildren, nine thousand great-grandchildren, eighty-six thousand great-great-grand-children, and I don't know how many great-great-great- and great-great-great-great-grandchildren, and I've only seen two Dogs in my life...both at a distance."

"See, Bean?" said Lugsy, yawning. Even the smell of the sleeping potion was very powerful. "I wish you'd stop pretending all the time."

"That doesn't mean that young Bean was pretending," Grannie went on. "But on the other paw, Bean loves to imagine things." Grannie leaned down close to Bean. "You're not a giant fire-breathing dragon, you know. You're just a little bunny." She leaned even closer, tapping Bean on the nose. "At least that's what you are on the *outside*. Get it?" Bean looked up at Grannie, confused. But she was already rummaging in one of her cabinets.

"Pickled parsnips, wasn't it?" she said, handing Lugsy an acornful.

"Come on." Lugsy turned to Bean, who had been leaning dreamily over the pot of sleeping potion. "We've got to get going. Mother's waiting."

The three bunnies scampered out of Grannie's kitchen and headed toward home.

Before too long, just two bunnies were scampering. One was hopping slowly. Grannie's sleeping potion was strong, and Bean was feeling very tired. He was so tired, in fact, that when he reached a soft clump of dandelions, he fell down in a heap and started to snooze.

Meanwhile, the Dog was back at the farmhouse practicing the best way to chase bunnies. He whirled around, barked a bunny-scaring bark, and then ran smack into a tall pair of legs that could belong to only one person — the mean old Farmer.

"What are you doing, you stupid beast?" The Farmer's angry voice came from far above the Dog's head.

The Dog whimpered, sniveled, shivered, and shook. He was very, very frightened of the Farmer.

"You see this?" The Farmer dropped a half-eaten head of lettuce onto the ground.

"This lettuce has been eaten by rabbits! Rabbits, you brainless hound! They've been in the garden again! Ah-ah-choooooo! Ah-choooo!"

The Farmer pulled out his pocket handkerchief and blew his nose loudly. "You know I'm allergic to rabbits," he went on, waving his handkerchief at the Dog. "Oooooh, they make me sneeze something awful! Your job is to get rid of those rabbits. Understand? And while you're at it, bring me a couple to put in the stew. The only good rabbit is a stewed rabbit. Ah-choooo!"

The Farmer sneezed so hard that a button popped right off his pants. "Another button!" bellowed the Farmer. "Those blasted rabbits!" He stomped off, sneezing as he went.

The Dog slunk off in the other direction, his tail dragging. "There's only one thing to do," he finally decided. "I've got to get those bunnies!"

Bean Bunny was still fast asleep in the dandelion patch, having a wonderful dream. He was dreaming that he was a giant skunk. No Dog would go anywhere near him. Deep in dreamland, he didn't hear the rustle in the tall grasses, and he didn't see a wet, black nose poke through. It was the nose of the Dog.

A bunny! the Dog thought excitedly. *A bunny! I must think about what to do. Yes, think. Think. Think.*

Thinking was not easy for the Dog.

If I chase this bunny, he will run away. So…this time, I will follow the bunny. That way, he will lead me to all the other bunnies!

The Dog was so proud of himself for thinking all this that he patted himself on the head. Then he lay down to wait until the bunny woke up.

A few moments later, Bean was awakened by a loud snoring noise. "What's that?" he wondered, stretching. He peeked through the dandelions in the direction of the sound and saw the sleeping Dog.

Bean took off in a flash. Gasping for breath, his heart pounding, he raced to warn the others.

When the Dog woke up, Bean was nowhere to be seen.

"Oh, moan!" the Dog moaned. "No bunny!"

Then he noticed a patch of blue tangled up in the dandelions. It was Bean's scarf. In his hurry to escape, the bunny had left it behind.

"Sniff, sniff!" The Dog sniffed the scarf excitedly. "The bunny is gone, but his scent is still here! If I follow the scent, I will find the bunny!"

The Dog was so proud of himself for thinking all this that he patted himself on the head again. Then he sniffled and snurfled after the scent and set off in search of the bunnies.

Hundreds of bunnies had gathered in the clearing for the opening ceremonies of the Bunny Picnic. Hind legs tapped impatiently, and noses quivered. They could hardly wait for the festivities to begin.

"Ahem." Mayor Bunnyparte cleared his throat. "Now that the storyteller is here, it is my official duty as Mayor of this warren officially to declare the Bunny Picnic officially started! And in the official tradition of Bunny Picnicdom, the first official event will be the storyteller's tale!"

All the bunnies cheered.

"Ahem." The storyteller cleared his throat. "This year," he began, "I'm going to tell you the Tale of the Giant Hedgehog!"

"My favorite!" whispered Lugsy.

That's when Bean burst into the circle of bunnies and ran straight for his big brother.

"Lugsy! Lugsy!" he said, pulling on Lugsy's sleeve. "There's a —"

"Not now, Bean!" Lugsy whispered. "You'll ruin the story."

"Once upon a time," the storyteller began, "there was a nasty old fox who loved to eat hedgehogs."

"Lugsy! Lugsy! I saw a Dog!" Bean insisted.

"If you saw a Dog, then where is it?" Lugsy asked. Bean looked around. There was no sign of the Dog.

"One day," the storyteller went on, "the nasty old fox fell asleep right in the middle of the forest. Suddenly, he was awakened by a mysterious voice. He looked up and saw a huge figure standing in front of him. 'Fox! Fox!' the voice said. 'I'm the giant hedgehog! But even though I'm really, really big and you're really, really little, I'm not going to hurt you. And do you know why?'"

For a moment, Bean forgot all about the Dog. He was imagining that he was the giant hedgehog.

"'N-n-n-o, w-w-w-why?' asked the fox, who was so frightened that the red fur on his tail turned white.

"'Because THEY WHO HURT OTHERS HURT THEMSELVES!'

"With that, the giant hedgehog disappeared, as mysteriously as he'd arrived. And the nasty old fox never ate another hedgehog again."

"Yaaaaaay!" the bunnies all cheered.

"I just love that part," Lugsy said, clapping hard.

"Lugsy! Shhhh!" Bean had remembered the Dog again. He tugged at his brother's sleeve. "The Dog will hear us!"

"For the last time, Bean, there is no Dog!" Lugsy snapped. Then he was interrupted by a loud noise.

"Bark bark bark! Growl! Woof! Woof!"

"A Dog?" yelled Father.

"A Dog!" Lugsy gasped.

Before anyone could say *Dog* again, the Dog himself jumped right into the middle of the group of terrified bunnies.

"Run!" yelled Mayor Bunnyparte. All the bunnies raced for the safety of the burrow.

Later that night, Mother tucked Bean, Lugsy, and
Twitch into their beds. The Dog was still wandering
around outside.

"Oh, Mother." Twitch sighed. "When can we have the
Bunny Picnic?"

"No one puts a paw out of the burrow until that Dog is
gone for good," Mother said sternly. "Good-night, Twitch,
good-night, Lugsy."

"Good-night, Mother," came two sad bunny voices.

"Good-night, Bean," Mother said, tucking Bean's
covers a little tighter.

"I'm not Bean," came a muffled voice from under the
pillow. "I'm a giant hedgehog."

"Well, then…good-night, giant hedgehog." Mother sighed.

"Good-night," said Bean. Then Mother turned off the light and shut the door.

Suddenly, Bean felt a soft something hit his bed. It was Lugsy's pillow.

"It's bad enough to miss the picnic without you pretending to be a stupid giant hedgehog!" whispered Lugsy angrily.

Bean had had enough. "I am not a stupid giant hedgehog. I am a clever giant hedgehog. And you know why? Because I was right about the Dog. You'd be a giant hedgehog, too, if you could!"

Lugsy opened his mouth to reply when Twitch stopped him. "Bean is right," she said. "Even I'd be a giant hedgehog if it meant we'd get rid of the Dog and have the picnic."

"You'd be a giant hedgehog, too?" Bean asked. A strange picture was forming in his mind. "Wait a minute. Wait a minute…."

"We're waiting." Lugsy snorted impatiently.

"I've got an idea!" Bean was so excited he fell out of bed.

Lugsy snorted again, but Bean paid no attention to him. He began to explain his idea. It took some time to describe, but when Bean had finished, even Lugsy had to admit that it just might work.

The three bunnies slid out of bed, dressed as quietly as they could, and slipped out of their burrow. Then they scurried up and down tunnels, waking all their friends — Babble and Snort and Bulbus and Bebop and all the other little bunnies — and told them about Bean's plan.

The rest of the night was filled with bunny activity. The bunnies measured and marked and snipped and sewed until it was light. Then it was time for someone to go across the meadow to Great-great-great-great-grandmother's house to get some sleeping potion. Lugsy volunteered.

While Bebop, Bulbous, Babble, and Snort kept the Dog busy, poking their noses out of the burrow and calling him silly names, Lugsy sneaked out. As soon as he was safely away from the Dog, he ran to Grannie's.

"Bean, why don't you climb to the top of the tree and thump when Lugsy comes back?" Twitch suggested.

So Bean scampered up the trunk of the oak tree that grew near the entrance to the burrow.

He watched, and he waited. Finally, he saw Lugsy, carrying the sleeping potion.

"He's here! He's here!" Bean was so excited that he called at the top of his voice and thumped as hard as he could.

All the bunnies heard him.

So did the Dog.

"He's here? Who's here? Bunny?" The Dog looked around, and immediately caught sight of Lugsy.

"Oh, no!" Bean screamed. "Lugsy! Run!"

But it was too late. The Dog pounced on Lugsy and caught the poor bunny in his paws.

"Oh, no, oh, no!" Bean cried. "It's all my fault! The Dog's got Lugsy! This is the most horrible, awful, terrible thing of all!"

Bean and the other bunnies watched in horror as Lugsy squirmed in the Dog's paws.

"I've got a bunny! I've got a bunny!" the Dog barked gleefully.

At that moment, Lugsy splashed the sleeping potion right into the Dog's face.

The Dog had just enough time to put Lugsy in his big brown sack. Then he fell flat on his stomach and started to snore. Unfortunately, he was still clutching the sack in his paws.

"I should have been a giant rock," moaned Bean. "Then I couldn't have moved or shouted, and Lugsy would be safe!"

"Never mind that," Twitch said. "There's no time to waste. If we're going to rescue Lugsy, we've got to go ahead with our plan. And we need you to get on top."

"But I can't!" Bean quaked with fear. "I'm…I'm…I'm a giant rock, and I don't even move!"

He closed his mouth and sat perfectly still…except
for his tail, which was still trembling.

"What about Lugsy?" Twitch said simply.

Bean shivered and shook. But deep down inside, he
knew he had to help his big brother.

"Okay," he finally said, taking a deep breath. "I'll do it.
I'll get on top."

When the Dog finally woke up, he yawned a great yawn.

Then he remembered the sack in his paws. He looked down at it and grinned.

"I've got a bunny for the Farmer's stew!" he barked happily.

That's when he saw a huge, strange thing towering over him.

"What?" The Dog rubbed his eyes. "Who are you?"

"I am the giant bunny," said Bean in his deepest voice.

Indeed, that's just what Bean looked like. He and all the other bunnies were inside the giant bunny costume they had stayed up all night snipping and sewing. Bean had gotten the idea for the costume from the storyteller's tale about the giant hedgehog. Only when he'd gotten the idea, he hadn't planned on being at the top of the costume doing all the talking.

"Oh, no!" The Dog's eyes grew wider and wider. "A giant bunny! Oh, please don't hurt me, giant bunny!"

"It's working!" Twitch whispered from underneath Bean.

"Please hurry," snorted Snort, who was on the very bottom. "My knees are going to break!"

"I WON'T HURT YOU, DOG," Bean said loudly. "AND DO YOU KNOW WHY?"

"No," the Dog said. "Why?"

"BECAUSE...." Bean took a deep breath. "THEY WHO HURT OTHERS HURT THEMSELVES! SO LET GO OF THAT BUNNY YOU HAVE IN YOUR BAG!"

The Dog opened the sack in a flash, and out fell Lugsy. The bunny took one look at the Dog and ran for his life.

"I really hate to lose that bunny," the Dog sniffed sadly. "The Farmer wanted him for a stew."

"A stew?" Bean gasped. He started to shake all over.

"Bean, no!" Twitch whispered. But it was too late. All the other bunnies had started to shake, too, and the giant bunny costume began to sway back and forth. Then, faster than it takes to say, "Easy-peasy-one-two-threesy," Bean tumbled off Twitch's shoulders. The giant bunny costume collapsed and fell into a heap on the grass, and all the little bunnies ran desperately for places to hide.

Just then, a deep voice called from the lettuce patch.
"Where are you, you miserable mongrel, you worth-
less mutt of a dog? Ah-chooo! Ah-chooooo!"

"Oh, no!" The Dog buried his face in his paws and
began to sob. "The Farmer's coming, and I don't have
any bunnies! He's going to beat me. I just know it!"

Bean was so astonished to hear the horrible, awful, terrible Dog crying that he crawled out of his hiding place and moved closer to get a better look.

"Oh, whimper, whimper!" the Dog whimpered. "What am I to do?"

Bean stared and stared. Then, after a moment, he called out to the Dog. "Hey! You're afraid of the Farmer, aren't you? Even though you're a giant Dog."

The Dog nodded, sniffling. "Oh please, oh please, someone save me!" he moaned.

Bean knew what it was like to be afraid. Suddenly, the Dog looked a little less horrible, awful, and terrible.

"I'll save you!" Bean decided. "Quick. Hide in here!" Bean pushed the Dog into a big bush and jumped in after him.

"Where is that wretched — ah-ah-ah-ah-chooo!" the Farmer sneezed as he stomped into the clearing.

"What's going on?" Bean whispered to the Dog.

"Bunnies make him sneeze something awful!" the Dog whispered back.

"They do? Hmmmm." Bean's eyes lit up. "That gives me another idea." Bean took three deep breaths and crawled out from under the bush. Then he marched right up to the Farmer.

"Oh, ah-ah-ah-ah-ah-chooooooo!" the Farmer sneezed. "Stay away from me, or I'll — ah-chooooo!"

"Come on, everybunny!" Bean called. "Out in the open!"

"Ah-ah-ah-choooo!" sneezed the Farmer.

When they realized what was going on, all the other bunnies hopped bravely up to Bean.

"Ah-ah-ah-ah-ah-chooooo!" the Farmer sneezed again. Then — pop! — another button popped off his trousers. "Ah-ah-ah-choo!" Still another button flew off. And "Ah-ah-ah-choo!" The last button popped, and the Farmer's trousers fell right down to his ankles!

"Blasted bunnies!" the Farmer gasped. "I give up! I'm going to sell this old farm and move back to the city!" Sneezing and wheezing, he stumbled away from the warren.

As soon as he was gone, a great cheer went up. "Yaaaay!" all the bunnies shouted.

Then the Dog slid out from under the bush. "Oh, moan," he moaned. "I'm glad to see that Farmer gone, but what is to become of me? Where will I live? How will I eat?"

Bean looked at the Dog. He still didn't look so horrible, awful, or terrible. He looked like someone in need of a friend. "Well, I suppose you can stay here with us," Bean said shyly.

"Really? May I?" the Dog begged. "I won't be any trouble, I promise!"

"Bean!" Lugsy poked his brother. "He can't stay here! He's a giant Dog!"

"So what?" Bean said. "I was just a giant bunny!"

Lugsy looked at his little brother for a long time. "You're right," he said finally. "You were a giant bunny." Lugsy raised his voice. "If my little brother says the Dog can stay here, then the Dog can stay here!"

When all the other bunnies heard what had happened, they gathered to congratulate Bean and to get a good look at the not-so-horrible, not-so-awful, not-so-terrible Dog. Then Mayor Bunnyparte officially declared that the Bunny Picnic could officially begin again. The storyteller made up a new story especially for the occasion — the story of Bean and the Giant Bunny. After he told it, the Dog clapped the hardest of all, and Bean turned pink with pride.

Great-great-great-great-grandmother had been right. Bean might look like a little bunny on the *outside*, but on the *inside*, he was a big, brave bunny. In fact, Bean was the hero of the Bunny Picnic!